SUSAN FARRINGTON

WHAT I LOVE about YOU

WITHDRAWN

BALZER+BRAY

AN IMPRINT OF HARPERCOLLINSPUBLISHERS

Do you know what I love?

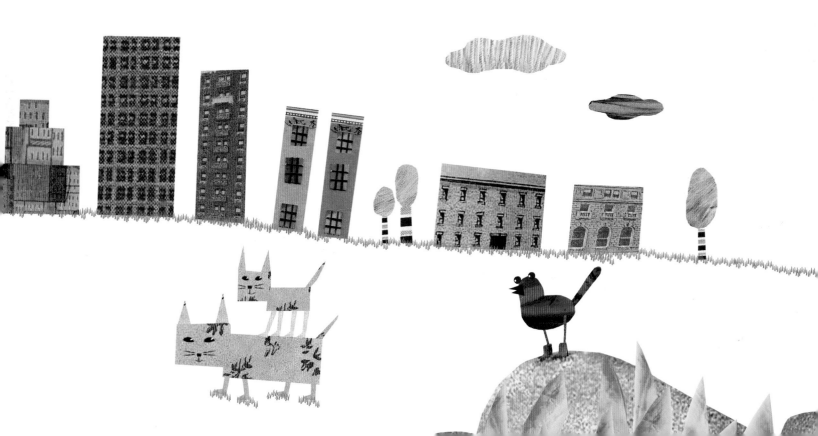

I love when you

SMILE.

Right before you
SING
at the top of your lungs.

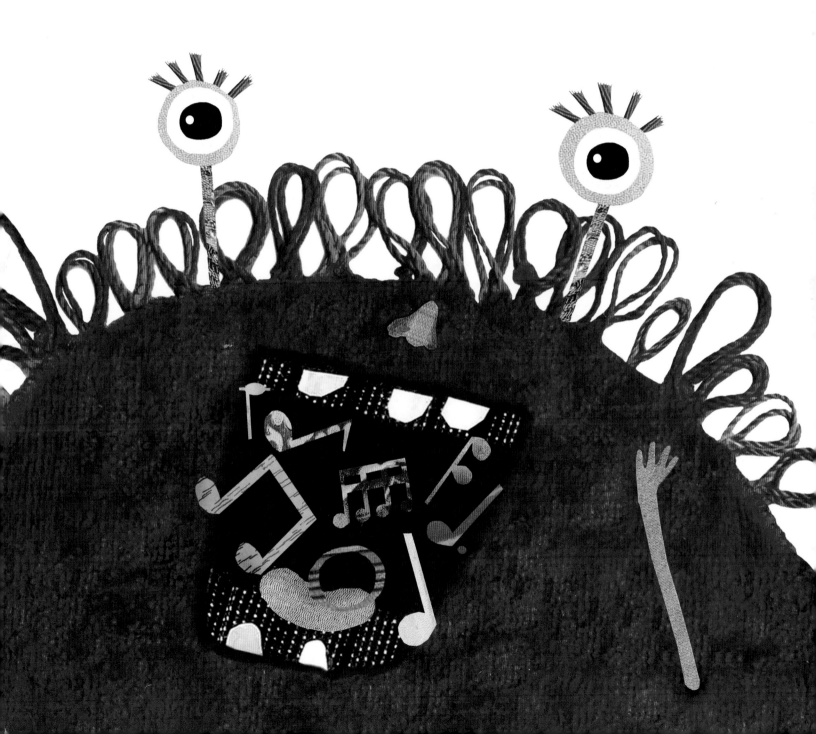

Do you know what I love?

I love when you're CREATIVE.

Even when things get
MESSY.

Do you know what I love?

I love when you
hold my hand.

And when you let go to
make new friends.

Do you know what I love?

I love when you're **KIND.**

And when you're

SILLY.

Do you know what I love?

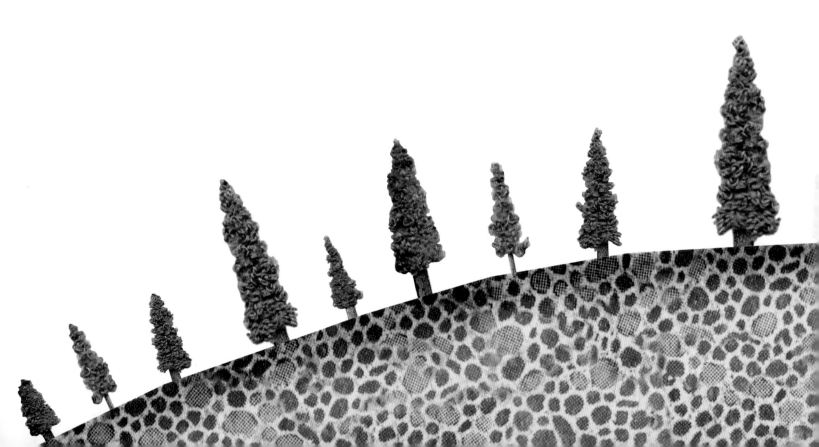

I love when you're
BRAVE.

And when you find me if
you need help.

Do you know what I love?
I love when we stay up late
to **READ** stories.

And when you get a good night's sleep.

Do you know
WHO I love?

I LOVE YOU!

To my wonderful mom and dad, Lucille and Paul Farrington.
Thanks for showing me how it's done.

And to my family—Steve, Kiley, and Julia Owen.
I could fill a book with what I love about you.

Balzer + Bray is an imprint of HarperCollins Publishers.

What I Love about You
Copyright © 2016 by Susan Farrington

ISBN 978-0-06-239353-1 (trade bdg.)

Book design by Alison Donalty
16 17 18 19 20 SCP 10 9 8 7 6 5 4 3 2 1
❖ First Edition